BURGHEAD PRIMARY SCHOOL

Roy Apps
the tWITCHES on HORRIDAY

Illustrated by Carla Daly

SIMON & SCHUSTER
YOUNG BOOKS

Text copyright © 1991 Roy Apps
Illustrations copyright © 1991 Carla Daly

First published in Great Britain in 1991
by Simon & Schuster Young Books

Reprinted in 1992, 1993

Photoset in 14pt Meridien by Goodfellow & Egan Ltd, Cambridge
Color origination by Scantrans Pte Ltd, Singapore

Printed and bound in Portugal by Edições ASA

Simon & Schuster Young Books
Campus 400
Maylands Avenue
Hemel Hempstead, Herts HP2 7EZ

BRITISH LIBRARY CATALOGUING IN PUBLICATION DATA
Apps, Roy
  The Twitches
  I. Title   II. Daly, Carla   III. Series
823'.914 [J]

ISBN 0 7500 1012 6
ISBN 0 7500 1013 4 (pbk)

"Come to Gertie-Wertie, little warty toad . . ." Gert put on her sweetest, softest voice, but it still came out like a cackle of an old crow.

This was hardly surprising, because she and her twin sister Lil were twitches, that is, they were *twins* who were also *witches*.

They were crawling on their scrawny hands and knobbly knees through their overgrown garden, hunting for a nice, fat, juicy, warty toad for supper.

5

"Don't know why you can't make do with tinned toad," muttered Lil.

"Because *I* have *taste*, crab-face," snorted Gert.

"Croak!" came a sound like a enormous burp.

"Manners Gert, please," snapped Lil.

"That wasn't me, you old twitch!" hissed Gert.

"Croak!"

A great big warty toad sprang out from under a dock leaf.

"There he goes, Lil!"

Crashing through the bindweed and brambles they went, the warty toad leaping from left to right, a few paces in front of them.

With one extra long bound it leapt right over the hedge and out of the garden.

With one extra long bound Gert and Lil leapt right over the hedge after it and –

"Aaaargh!!!!!"

Thump.

"Yeoww!!!"

– landed straight on the back of a passing lorry.

But not just any old passing lorry. For when Gert and Lil finished rubbing their bruises they looked round and saw that with them were a Roman general, four Martians, two pirates and Count Dracula.

CHAPTER TWO

The lorry turned into the recreation ground and
screeched to halt by a big marquee.

"Curse this lorry!" fumed Lil.

"Good idea," agreed Gert. "Let's turn all the petrol
into bat's blood!"

Suddenly, a very large, fat man wearing a
glittering gold chain around his neck clambered on
to the back of the lorry.

"It's the Mayor!" gasped Gert.

And so it was. He was followed by a short, fat little
man in a grey suit. The Mayor looked from the
Martians to the pirates to the Roman general to
Count Dracula and then his eyes finally rested on
Gert and Lil.

"Oh yes, oh yes, oh yes, oh yes," he said, and turning to the short, fat man in the grey suit added, "the witches are far and away the best."

The short, fat man wriggled and looked extremely uncomfortable. "Are you sure, your Worship?" he whispered anxiously to the Mayor. "I don't like the look of them one bit. How about that Count Dracula, he seems a nice lad?"

"Rubbish, Herbert," chortled the Mayor. And without further ado, he cleared his throat and announced: "As Mayor of this town, it is my great privilege to award first prize in this year's Summer Carnival Fancy Dress competition to the witches!" And he pinned a bright red rosette on Gert and Lil's black hats.

"You *twerp*," cackled Lil, "we haven't entered any comp– *Yeowww*!" she yelled as Gert kicked the boniest part of her very bony ankle.

"Er . . . What *is* the prize?" asked Gert with a glint in her greedy eye. "Is it lots and lots of money?"

"Oh no," said the Mayor. "It's an all expenses paid, fortnight's holiday in Spain, with Mr Herbert Sherbert here," – and he patted the short, fat little man on the head – "of Sherbert's Happy Holidays Limited. You will be staying at the magnificent Hotel Magnifico, owned by Mr Sherbert's cousin, Senor Alphonso Sherberto."

"Wow! Yuk!" beamed Gert.

"Phew! Putrid!" grinned Lil.

For these are witches' ways of saying that the idea of two weeks in Spain was a very attractive one indeed.

"I don't like the look of them, your Worship,"
hissed Herbert Sherbert.

"You're not meant to like the look of them!
They're in Fancy Dress. Aren't you?" the Mayor
asked Lil.

"Well," replied Lil doubtfully, "this is certainly a
dress, but I'd hardly call it *fancy*,"

"Can you get warty toads in Spain?" asked Gert
brightly.

And Herbert Sherbert turned as green as a lizard's
leg.

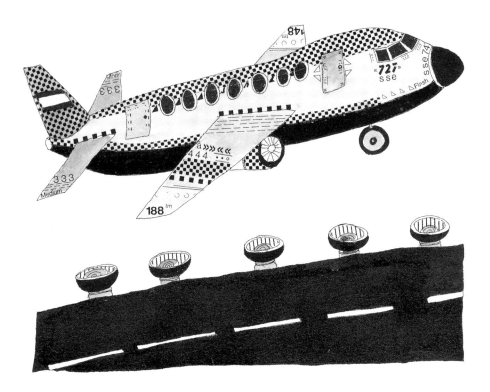

CHAPTER THREE

"Fasten your seat belts, we are about to land," crackled the Captain's voice over the loudspeaker.

The plane's tyres screeched as they hit the runway.

"Ooo-er, my ears have gone all funny," said Lil.

"They haven't *gone* all funny, they've always looked like that!" Gert laughed like an old hen with a megaphone.

All the passengers in the plane looked round to see what the dreadful noise was, while Herbert Sherbert slid further and further down his seat, trying to make himself invisible. "I told the Mayor they'd be trouble!" he muttered to himself.

Gert and Lil sat in the bus that was taking them from the airport to the Hotel Magnifico.

"Slithering frog's spawn, it *is* hot, isn't Lil?" exclaimed Gert.

And she took off her hat.

"Atchoo! Atchooo! Atchoooo!"

Immediately everybody on the bus started coughing and sneezing, for under Gert's hat were thirty six years' worth of dandruff, dust and cobwebs.

"*A-a-a-atch-o-o-o-o*!!!" went Lil.

"Why curse you, dear," cackled Gert, which is what witches say to each other when they sneeze.

Lil pulled the headrest cover off the seat in front and blew her nose into it – "*Paaaarpppp!*" – so loudly that the whole bus shook.

Everyone on the bus looked in horror at the twitches. Then they shot angry glances at Herbert Sherbert as if to say, "So, those disgusting old witches are with *you*, are they?"

And, of course, they were.

"Ah Herbert, welcome to the Hotel Magnifico!"

Senor Alphonso hugged his cousin until Herbert felt that all his breath had been squeezed out of him.

"And you ladies must be the Fancy Dress Competition winners!" Senor Alphonso's smile was so broad that his gold-capped teeth sparkled in the sun.

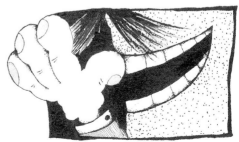

"How dare you, young man!" snarled Lil.

"Pardon?" exclaimed Senor Alphonso.

"Never in all my one hundred and thirteen and a quarter years have I been so insulted!" Lil went on. "Has no one ever taught you how to address your elders and betters?"

Now, it is very rude to call a witch a "lady". They much prefer it if you refer to them as "You Old Hag", or, if they are very important witches, "My Most Ancient Crone".

"Kindly address my sister and me as 'Madam Twitches'," she said, huffily. "Otherwise I'll curdle your blood into goat's yoghurt!"

"Er . . . of course, er . . . Madam Twitches," said Senor Alphonso, a little nervously. "They'd better not be any trouble!" he muttered under his breath to his cousin.

"You know, Gert, this looks a really scrummy menu," said Lil, as she and Gert sat down to dinner in the Hotel Magnifico's posh restaurant.

This is what the menu said:

MENU

for firsts

Toad-in-the-hole

for seconds

Mousse

"Senor Alphonso!" squawked Lil when her first course arrived. "What is *this*?" She prodded her toad-in-the-hole with a long and very grubby fingernail.

"Toad-in-the-hole."

"Well, I can't see any toad," complained Lil angrily.

A number of the other diners began to turn green and to look very ill indeed.

"And neither can I," added Gert. "What's this long round thing – it's not a slice of boiled snake is it?"

"That," said Senor Alphonso, shaking with anger, "is a sausage!"

"Then why does it say *toad* on your menu?" asked Lil. "My sister and I were looking forward to a nice fat, juicy, warty toad!"

"And another thing, young man!" boomed Gert.

Everyone turned round and Senor Alphonso froze on the spot.

"This *For Seconds*," Gert pointed to the menu, "is it dormouse or harvest mouse?"

Two ladies dining in the far corner screamed. And two gentlemen in the opposite corner fainted.

25

"It's not *mouse*!" yelled Senor Alphonso indignantly. "It's *mousse*! Strawberry mousse!"

"In that case," said Gert, acidly, "I'll just have a drink."

"A drink of what?" asked Senor Alphonso with a tremor.

"Oh, a small glass of slime juice will do," said Gert.

Several of the other diners rushed out clutching table napkins to their mouths.

"You . . . you disgusting old hags!" screamed Senor Alphonso in fury.

"Ah, you see, he likes us really," said Lil, with a black-toothed smile.

"Herbert!" snarled Senor Alphonso in his cousin's ear, "I want them out of my hotel and on the plane home, first thing in the morning!"

CHAPTER FOUR

"That was the most uncomfortable night I have ever spent in my life," said Lil grumpily next morning. "Those sheets had been *washed*, you know, I'm sure of it!"

"Urgh! I'll be glad to get back home to the hovel," said Gert. "That strange smell, what was it?"

"Soap, I think," said Lil, with great disgust.

There was a knock at the door and in came a

chambermaid, loaded with dusters, brushes and a vacuum cleaner. "Good morning, I've come to clean your room," she said brightly.

Gert and Lil screwed up their faces in horror.

"Language, please!" said Lil, in a shocked voice.

Suddenly, Gert's face broke out into a wide, toothless smile. "Have you got a spare broom?" she asked the chambermaid.

"We don't use brooms any more," replied the chambermaid, "we use this." She pointed to the vacuum cleaner. "It's a Whizzo Zoom."

"I thought we might as well take a trip before we go home," explained Gert to Lil, in a whisper. "See a bit of the countryside – we might even come across a warty toad or two."

"What, on this?" Lil eyed the Whizzo Zoom suspiciously.

"Why not? It's got a long handle, the same as a broomstick. Hop on."

Whooosh!

"Hey! Come back!" yelled the chambermaid.

But off went the Whizzo Zoom, with Gert and Lil clutching on to the handle.

Crash! went the potted fern on the landing, as they caught it a glancing blow.

"It's quite smooth, but not fast enough for my liking!" yelled Lil above the roar of the Whizzo Zoom.

"Left here," yelled Gert, as they reached the dining room door. And she put out her hand to signal.

Crash! went a full set of plates, bowls, cups and saucers as Gert's outstretched arm swept them off the crockery trolley.

On to the verandah they roared.

"Stop! You vandals! Stop!" screamed Senor
Alphonso, but Gert and Lil had no idea how to stop
the Whizzo Zoom.

Senor Alphonso stepped backwards as the Whizzo
Zoom hurtled towards him.

"Oo-er!" cried Lil, as she suddenly saw the hotel swimming pool in front of them.

Splash!

"Aaaaargh!" cried Senor Alphonso.

Splash!

"Glug . . . Glug . . ." went Gert.

"Glug . . . Glug . . ." went Lil.

"You . . .!" spluttered Senor Alphonso, as they all
bobbed up to the surface.

"Just thought, we'd *drop in*!" cackled Gert,
opening her mouth wide in a loud, toothless laugh.
For Gert's jokes, like her manners and her taste in
warty toads, were really, really bad.

"I told the Mayor they'd be trouble!" explained Herbert Sherbert to his cousin, as he came racing across to the swimming pool.

"Get them a plane home now!"

"I can't, Alphonso!"

"Can't? What do you mean can't?"

"The next plane doesn't leave until tomorrow!"

CHAPTER FIVE

"I'm not having you anywhere *near* my hotel!"
fumed a very wet Senor Alphonso. "You will stay
the night over there."

He led Gert and Lil out of the hotel courtyard and
across a field.

"And you, Herbert," he called over his shoulder to
his cousin, "you will pay for all the damage they
have done to my hotel!"

They arrived at a crumbling, tumbling-down old shed. "This is all *you're* fit for," said Senor Alphonso crossly. "It's where I used to keep my goats."

"Mmmmm, yes, so I can smell," sniffed Lil.

"Mmmmm, what a stink," sniffed Gert, happily. "This is more like it."

Herbert Sherbert gulped like a man who has swallowed a bag of marbles. "You *like* it in here?"

"Not half," said Gert, hugging herself. "It feels so . . . so *damp*. And *so* filthy!"

"And it looks as if there are plenty of spiders and cockroaches about," put in Lil. "Just you wait until we tell them all back home down at *The Hag's Head*."

"You mean . . . your friends would want to come and stay in my old goat house for their holidays?" asked Alphonso, doubtfully.

"Not holidays. Witches don't have holidays. They have *horrid*ays," explained Gert.

"'Sherbert's Hideous Horridays'. Mmmmm, I like it," mused Herbert.

"If the Twitches find the customers and I organize the travel . . . your goat shed could be fully booked all year round, Alphonso."

Senor Alphonso thought long and hard.
"Mmmmm, I wouldn't have to decorate. I wouldn't
have to pay a chambermaid to clean. There would be
no laundry bills. It wouldn't cost me *anything*!" he
exclaimed.

"You would have to let us have two weeks'
horriday a year, here, free," said Gert.

"And you would have to forget about charging me
for the damage the twitches did to the Hotel
Magnifico," added Herbert.

"Of course! Of course!" said Senor Alphonso,
beaming his best hotel manager's smile once again.

"What a good thing it was you two ladies er . . .
Madam Twitches who won the Fancy Dress
Competition."

"Exactly what I told the Mayor," said Herbert,
with his fingers crossed firmly behind his back.

That night in the goat's shed, Gert woke Lil with a start.

"Can you hear what I can hear?" she said.

Croak!

"A warty toad!" exclaimed Lil. "A nice, fat, juicy, warty toad! Where is it?"

"I can't see! It's dark."

"I think it's over there in the corner. Are you ready to pounce? After two, right?"

"Right."

"One. Two . . ."

AAAAAARRRRRGGGGGHHHHH!!!!!

Look out for other exciting new titles in the **Storybooks** series.

Babybug
Catherine Storr
Illustrated by Fiona Dunbar

When Tania's new baby brother arrives, she can't understand what all the fuss is about. He even has a baby alarm, so her parents can hear him crying when he's in another room! Then Tania has a wonderful idea – why not switch the alarm around so she can hear what her parents say when she's not in the room?

The Shoemaker's Boy
Joan Aiken
Illustrated by Alan Marks

When his father goes off on a pilgrimage, Jem is left in charge of the shoemaker's shop. This proves a bigger task than Jem had realised!

T.V. Genie
John Talbot

Paul isn't looking forward to staying with his grandad over the holidays. But he changes his mind when he discovers an old television set up in the attic. It's got black and white magic!

Seymour Finds a Home
Dyan Sheldon
Illustrated by Nigel McMullen

Seymour is a dragon with a problem. Whenever he tries to breathe fire, all that comes out is snow!

You can buy all these books from your local bookshop, or they can be ordered direct from the publishers. For more information about Storybooks write to The Sales Department, Simon & Schuster Young Books, Campus 400, Maylands Avenue, Hemel Hempstead HP2 7EZ.